I0578494

The Kitten Psychologist And What The Kitten Did

THEA VAN DIEPEN

OTHER WORKS

WHITE CHANGELING SERIES

Hidden In Sealskin
Like Mist Over The Eyes

THE UNDEAD FAIRY TALES
COLLECTION

The Illuminated Heart

Dreaming Of Her And Other Stories
The Tree Remembers

Find other works by the author at
https://www.theavandiepen.com

The Kitten Psychologist And What The Kitten Did

INKLETS #15

THEA VAN DIEPEN

Inkprint PRESS

www.inkprintpress.com

Copyright © 2019 Thea van Diepen
First published on the *Darkness & Good* blog
(darknessandgood.blogspot.com), February 2018.

All rights reserved. No part of this book may be
reproduced in any form or by any electronic or
mechanical means, including information storage
and retrieval systems, without permission in
writing from the publisher, except by a reviewer,
who may quote brief passages in a review.

This is a work of fiction. All characters,
organisations and events are the author's creation,
or are used fictitiously.

ISBN: 978-1-925825-14-5
eBook ISBN: 9781386307389

www.inkprintpress.com

*National Library of Australia Cataloguing-in-Publication
Data*
Van Diepen, Thea
The Kitten Psychologist And What The Kitten Did
26 p.
ISBN: 978-1-925825-14-5
Inkprint Press, Canberra, Australia
1. Fiction—Animals 2. Fiction—Short Stories

First Print Edition: August 2019
Cover design © Inkprint Press
Interior art © Amy Laurens

THE KITTEN PSYCHOLOGIST AND WHAT THE KITTEN DID

WEDNESDAY ARRIVED, AND 2:55PM found me in my office, sweating.

I've really got to turn the heat down in this place.

Oh.

It was down.

Well, crap.

I'd cancelled my other appointments that day when it became clear partway through my *first* one that all I could think about was *this* one. This one in thirty minutes.

My lunch tried to regurgitate itself. It did an excellent job.

4 out of 5 carrot-flavoured lumps for effort.

Who knew a kitten would be so much trouble?

...I did.

And I went for it anyways.

And now I'm here.

Was the thermostat actually working, or just pretending to work?

I simultaneously wished the kitten's owners would come early, and that they'd never come at all. Between ripping this experience off like a bandaid and waking up to find it all a dream... I honestly didn't know which one would be better.

Maybe the bandaid.

I sighed.

Yeah, it was the bandaid.

2:57.

What if I didn't show up? I could escape out the window, right? Three stories wouldn't be hard to climb down. I was sure it wouldn't be.

2:58.

My knee bobbed like a squirrel on cocaine. When had that started? *Stop that. Stop it.* Gah. Now the other one was doing it.

2:58.

Still?

Agh.

Okay, this is ridiculous. Pull yourself together. Or at least pretend to.

The door opened.

I jumped.

The kitten entered first, followed by Worn Jeans and Green Shirt.

Oh dear lord.

I licked my lips.

Had I had enough to drink today? My mouth was undergoing desertification.

"Hello," I said. Cleared my throat.

"Tell the psychologist what you told us," Worn Jeans demanded of the kitten.

'The psychologist.' Ouch.

"I went to the bank," the kitten said as it leapt onto my desk and sat primly, wrapping it tail around itself.

I blinked. "You what?"

"We've obviously got to supervise it more," said Worn Jeans, arms crossed.

"Wait, wait," I said, holding up my hands. "Two months ago, your kitten was too afraid to go outside. Period."

"It was?" asked Green Shirt. "I didn't know that."

Both of my friends had been sitting tensely and, due to my nerves, I hadn't noticed until now as they both… softened? Not much, but enough to remind me to listen. To focus.

I took a deep breath.

"Well, I'm not now," said the kitten. "Obviously." Its usual arrogance faltered for a split second when it glanced at its owners, but it soon regained its composure. "Since the source of all our arguments seems to be money and how to get it, it followed that I should start by opening a bank account. However I end up acquiring money, I must have some place to put it first. And let us not forget that this all started because I was paying you out of an account not my own. It was the logical course of action."

Never mind Voldemort. Now I was dealing with Spock. Or Spocklemort? Voldepock? "So you have an account now."

"Of course not. The idiot banker refused to open one for me."

"Because you're a cat."

"Because I have no money. And I'm underage." The kitten scoffed. "Underage. The whole system's felinist. I needed to be accompanied by a parent or guardian, apparently. Which my humans refuse to do for me. Neither will they lend me any money with which to make my first deposit."

I raised an eyebrow. "Can you blame them?"

The kitten eyed its owners. "I suppose not. But still. I'm trying to be responsible, here. You would think they'd see that."

"And how are you supposed to pay back your loan, exactly?" asked Worn Jeans.

"I'm working on that!" the kitten retorted.

I made what I hoped was a placating gesture to both of them. "I'm confused. Why are you talking to me about this?"

"Don't you see?" Worn Jeans' hands jabbed the air. "It went to the bank. On its own."

"Why is this even a problem?" Green Shirt exploded.

What the what now?

The kitten and I exchanged glances, but said nothing.

"Honey…" Worn Jeans said.

"No, really," Green Shirt continued, "why do we need to make a big deal about this? So it went to the bank to open an account. That's not a crime."

Worn Jeans scowled. "And whose money will it fill that account with? Ours?"

The kitten flicked its tail.

"It's going to pay us back. It said it would."

"It stole money from us for weeks, why would we believe what it said? And why does a kitten need money?"

"Because your friend needed help!" the kitten yelled.

Oh. Well. That changes things a bit.

THE MAKING OF
THE KITTEN
PSYCHOLOGIST AND
WHAT THE KITTEN DID

The series sat for a couple years after the previous instalment. Chilling. Unfinished. Frustrating. I'd ended it on a cliffhanger and had absolutely no idea what happened next, only that the kitten had done something that was, I assumed, egregious.

And it sat not because I couldn't come up with ideas of how to continue. I had plenty of them. Many were awful, true, but plenty nonetheless. The problem was that, when I sat down to write, writing didn't happen. I couldn't seem to get my fingers to do the thing.

Until one day, the switch flipped and I found myself sitting in front of my computer, able to write again.

My current working theory is that trying to write this part earlier had been me forcing something to happen that wasn't ready yet. Like I had to process some stuff before I'd be able to sit in on my next therapy session with me and my writing.

When I could finally write it, I didn't realize what had changed, but in re-reading the story to write about how I wrote it, I figured it out.

I needed a new perspective on what I'd been looking at for so long. I needed to allow the characters to have layers. To have hidden things.

I'd gone into these stories thinking it would help me solve what I was working through by giving me something new, or changing something that wasn't working for me. And while I started this instalment of the series thinking that I would be going down those same lines again, some part of me was finally ready to see that I already had what I needed. Hidden, but ready to be revealed.

And it was time to admit that it was there.

DOWNLOAD YOUR FREE EBOOK

When you buy a print book from Inkprint Press, we like to say THANK YOU by offering you the ebook for free!

Please head to www.inkprintpress.com/inklets/15/ and the use the coupon INK15 to get your copy of this Inklet in epub AND mobi today!
(Coupon will only work once.)

READ MORE!

DREAMING OF HER AND OTHER STORIES

A collection of short stories and poetry, written as refreshers, reminders of what makes life beautiful. Pieces include a story of the life of a river as he discovers his true self, a poetic retelling of Daphne's flight from Apollo, and, in the titular story, a literal nightmare as a girl comes to terms with the death of her sister.

https://www.theavandiepen.com

ABOUT THE AUTHOR

THEA VAN DIEPEN spent the first ten years of her life on a tree-wrapped acreage where an inquisitive child might believe in magic. Nowadays, she lives in Edmonton, breathing life into stories in the form of books such as the *White Changeling* series, a webcomic, and a video game.

Her website is theavandiepen.com, where she can be contacted in English and French... so long as you don't ask her to count in French, as she tends to miss numbers ending in six entirely by accident.

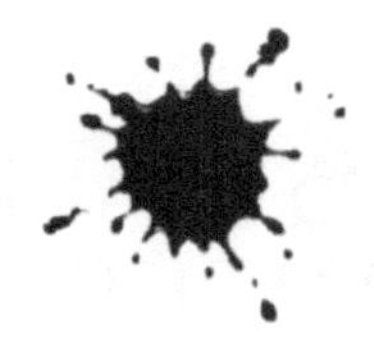

INKLETS

Collect them all! Released on the 1st and 15th of each month.

INKLET #007
SEVENTY
LIANA BROOKS

INKLET #008
A Final Request for Mercy
AMY LAURENS

INKLET #009
the kitten psychologist
vs
the kitten's owners
THEA VAN DIEPEN

INKLET #010
Answer the Question
AMY LAURENS

INKLET #011
Happily, Red
AMY LAURENS

INKLET #012
the kitten psychologist
tries to be patient
through email
THEA VAN DIEPEN

INKLET #013
DRAGON Tuesday
AMY LAURENS

INKLET #014
RED PLANET REFUGEES
LIANA BROOKS

INKLET #015
the kitten psychologist &
What The Kitten Did
THEA VAN DIEPEN

Cherry
Blossom
AMY LAURENS

Alone
AMY LAURENS

the kitten psychologist
& The Kitten
Come To A Conclusion
THEA VAN DIEPEN

LEVEL NINE
LIANA BROOKS

To Dust
AMY LAURENS

Interchange
AMY LAURENS

Emalia's
Lanterns
LIANA BROOKS

Dear Santa
AMY LAURENS

The
Quilt-Maker's
Scrap
AMY L. LAURENS

www.ingramcontent.com/pod-product-compliance
Lightning Source LLC
Chambersburg PA
CBHW051303190726
48286CB00004B/1249